DANDELION

To Lucas Lackner

# DANDELION

STORY AND PICTURES BY

## Don Freeman

### PUFFIN BOOKS

PUFFIN BOOKS
Published by the Penguin Group
Penguin Putnam Books for Young Readers,
345 Hudson Street, New York, New York 10014, U.S.A.
Penguin Books Ltd, 27 Wrights Lane, London W8 5TZ, England
Penguin Books Australia Ltd, Ringwood, Victoria, Australia
Penguin Books Canada Ltd, 10 Alcorn Avenue, Toronto, Ontario, Canada M4V 3B2
Penguin Books (N.Z.) Ltd, 182-190 Wairau Road, Auckland 10, New Zealand
Penguin Books Ltd, Registered Offices: Harmondsworth, Middlesex, England

**First published by The Viking Press 1964**
**Viking Seafarer Edition published 1968**
**Reprinted 1970, 1971, 1972, 1975**
**Published in Picture Puffins 1977**
47 49 50 48
**Copyright © Don Freeman, 1964**
**All rights reserved**

Library of Congress Cataloging in Publication Data
Freeman, Don.   Dandelion.
Summary: Dandelion overdresses for a come-as-
you-are party and is turned away because the
hostess does not recognize him.
[1. Lions—Fiction]  I. Title. PZ7.F8747Dan7 ( )  [E]
77-2562   ISBN 978-0-14-050218-3

Manufactured in China

**Set in Palatino**

On a sunny Saturday morning Dandelion woke up, stretched and yawned, and jumped out of bed.

After doing his daily exercises Dandelion looked out of the window, blinked his eyes, and said, "I wonder if the mail has come?"

He put on his sweater and went outside to the mailbox. There was a letter, and it was written in fancy gold ink!

Dear Dandelion:
You are invited to my tea-and-taffy party on Saturday afternoon at half-past three.
Come as you are.
Sincerely,
Jennifer Giraffe

Dandelion was very excited. "Why, that's today!" he said. "It's a good thing I planned to get a haircut!"

As soon as he had washed and dried the breakfast dishes and made his bed nice and neat, he ran down the street to the barbershop.

Lou Kangaroo had a chair waiting for him. First he trimmed Dandelion's hair, and

then gave him a shampoo.

Dandelion thought he should have a manicure too.

When Lou Kangaroo had finished Dandelion looked a bit foolish.
His mane was frizzy and fuzzy and completely unrulish.

"Maybe a wave would help," Lou suggested, showing him a picture in the latest fashion magazine for lions.

Dandelion agreed. This was exactly what he needed.

So Lou went about curling his mane.

He looked magnificent!

But now Dandelion thought he really should wear something more elegant than a sweater to the party.

"This jacket is the very newest style," said Theodore the Tailor, "and it just fits you. All you need now is a cap and a cane.

Happy Crane will be glad to help you."

What a dapper dandy he had suddenly become!

"It's nearly half-past three!" said Dandelion. "I've just time to get something for my hostess!"

A bouquet of dandelions would be perfect.

He knew this tall door very well, having been here many times before.

He rang the bell.

When Jennifer Giraffe opened the door
she looked very surprised. "Yes?" she said.
"What can I do for you?"

"Why, I've come to your party," he answered.

"Oh, I'm sorry, sir, but you are not anyone I know!" said Miss Giraffe.
"You must have come to the wrong address."

And with this she closed the door right in poor Dandelion's face!

"I'm Dandelion!" he roared. "You've made a mighty mistake!" But there was no use knocking. The door stayed tight shut.

Dandelion began walking back and forth. Back and forth, up and down the long block he paced.

And as he paced, the sky grew dark. Then a sudden gust of wind **sprang** up and blew away his beautiful bouquet, and his snappy cap flew off!

To make matters worse, it began to rain in torrents. Dandelion dropped his cane and stood under a weeping willow tree.

But the rain poured down through the branches. Dandelion was soon soaking wet and his curls came unfurled.

He took off his jacket and hung it on a willow branch. Luckily he had kept on his sweater.

At last the rain stopped and the warm sunshine came beaming down.

Dandelion decided to sit on Jennifer Giraffe's front steps until his mane was dry.

While he sat there waiting he spied three dandelion flowers under the bottom step where they had been protected from the wind and the rain.

He picked the dandelions and said, "I think I will try again."

And he rang the bell.

"Well, well! If it isn't our friend Dandelion at last!" said Jennifer Giraffe. "We've been waiting for you for the past hour. I do hope you weren't caught in that awful cloudburst!"

Everyone at the party greeted him heartily.

Later on when all her guests were enjoying tea and taffy, Jennifer Giraffe told Dandelion about the silly-looking lion who had come to the door earlier.

Dandelion almost spilled his cup of tea as he reared back and laughed uproariously, "Oh, that was me! I was that silly-looking lion!"

Miss Giraffe was so flustered she got herself all tangled up in her long pearl necklace. "I do apologize for having closed the door on you!" she said blushing. "I promise never to do such a thing again!"

"And I promise you I will never again try to turn myself into a stylish dandy," said Dandelion as he sipped his tea. "From now on I'll always be just plain me!"